VIOLET THE SNOWGIRL

A STORY OF LOSS AND HEALING

Lisa L. Walsh

Illustrated by Wendy Leach

free spirit
PUBLISHING®

Library of Congress Cataloging-in-Publication Data
Names: Walsh, Lisa L., author. | Leach, Wendy, illustrator.
Title: Violet the snowgirl : a story of loss and healing / Lisa L. Walsh ; illustrated by Wendy Leach.
Description: Minneapolis, MN : Free Spirit Publishing Inc., [2020] | Audience: Ages 5–10.
Identifiers: LCCN 2020008140 (print) | LCCN 2020008141 (ebook) | ISBN 9781631985171 (hardcover) | ISBN 9781631985188 (pdf) | ISBN 9781631985195 (epub)
Subjects: CYAC: Snowmen—Fiction. | Loss (Psychology)—Fiction. | Brothers and sisters—Fiction.
Classification: LCC PZ7.1.W3582 Vio 2020 (print) | LCC PZ7.1.W3582 (ebook) | DDC [E]—dc23
LC record available at https://lccn.loc.gov/2020008140
LC ebook record available at https://lccn.loc.gov/2020008141

Reading Level Grade 2; Interest Level Ages 5–10;
Fountas & Pinnell Guided Reading Level L

Edited by Christine Zuchora-Walske
Cover and interior design by Shannon Pourciau

10 9 8 7 6 5 4 3 2 1
Printed in China
R18860720

Free Spirit Publishing Inc.
6325 Sandburg Road, Suite 100
Minneapolis, MN 55427-3674
(612) 338-2068
help4kids@freespirit.com
freespirit.com

FSC
www.fsc.org
MIX
Paper from
responsible sources
FSC® C144853

Free Spirit offers competitive pricing.
Contact edsales@freespirit.com for pricing information on multiple quantity purchases.

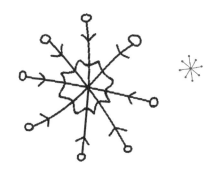

To my children.
Aleah and Hannah, you have endured
big changes with courage and great heart.
Daniel, you taught me that it is possible to love someone thoroughly,
long after they have parted from this world.

Jerzie woke up and opened her eyes. Then she remembered.
Today was the day after her birthday. This was always a boring day.

Every year, Jerzie's birthday arrived on a wave of party preparations.
Excitement built and built, until it crashed over her on one glorious day.
Then too quickly, it was over. She had to wait a whole year for the next birthday.

Jerzie took a breath and checked her feelings.
She felt sad. Her birthday cheer was gone.
The countdown of days, the visions of presents—*poof*!
Jerzie lay still in her warm, snuggly bed. She closed her eyes.

A soft knock interrupted Jerzie's thoughts.
Her chatty little brother probably wanted to do something boring.
"Go away, Josiah!" Jerzie grouched.

Jerzie looked out her window. She noticed fluffy snowflakes tumbling and twirling by.

The door slowly opened. As soon as she saw a purple coat and scarf though the crack, Jerzie's heart leapt—and so did she. *Grandma's here! Yay!*

"Good morning, sunshine!" said Grandma.
Jerzie sank her face into Grandma's cold coat.
Grandma smell, she thought happily.

After breakfast, Grandma, Jerzie, and Josiah stepped out into the courtyard.
The world was cold and crisp and white. Everything looked sparkly and new. Like magic.

Josiah stuck out his tongue to catch a huge snowflake. "Vanilla!" he announced,
laughing. Josiah and Grandma sampled the variety of snowflake flavors.
Jerzie fell backward to make a snow angel. The three took turns pulling one
another on the red sled.

The snow was sticky—perfect for snowballs. And a snowman! Jerzie rolled the fat bottom, Grandma made the middle, and Josiah formed the head.

Jerzie ran inside to find decorations. She came back outside carrying buttons for the eyes, a carrot for the nose, and a hat for the head.

Josiah had found two crooked sticks for the arms.
He poked the sticks in the snowman's sides. After all
the pieces were in place, Grandma wrapped her purple
scarf around the snowman's neck.

"Just right," she said.

The trio stepped back to admire their creation and made a surprising discovery. This was no snowman.

This was a snowgirl!

Josiah thought for a moment,
looking at the scarf.
"I know! Let's name her Purple!
Like Grandma's favorite color!"

"I like it!" Grandma said.
"But actually, my favorite color is
violet. Not only do I love the color,
but Violet was my mother's name."

"Yes! Violet the Snowgirl! And guess what? Violet is a pilot!" Jerzie said.

"And she will fly us straight to the moon," said Grandma.

"And we'll drink hot cocoa on a star," added Josiah. "Whipped cream for me, please!"

All day long, Violet was the center of their fun.

Violet became an alien creature and a third-grade teacher.

Violet was Granddad, a librarian, and a veterinarian.

Violet was brave, she was smart, and she showed her great heart.

Violet became anything they wanted her to be.

What a special day it was with Violet the Snowgirl.
Day turned to evening, and Jerzie, Josiah, and Grandma
played and laughed and sang by the light of the silver moon.
Their purple shadows danced on the snow.

The day after Jerzie's birthday turned out to be a great day.
Before she went to bed, Jerzie took a breath and checked her feelings again.
Her heart felt light. She was happy.

Grandma left on the train the next day. The weather stayed cold.
More snow fell, blanketing Violet.

One day the weather turned warm and it rained hard.
When Jerzie and Josiah got home from school, they
saw that Violet had melted into a mound of slush.

"Darn it. Darn it!" Josiah shouted.

He kicked the ground as hot tears streamed down his face.

"Why did she have to melt? I hate that snowgirl. Why did we ever make her?"

Mom was waiting for them with an umbrella. She wrapped Josiah in her arms and wiped his tears.
"I'm sorry you're so sad. It hurts," Mom said softly. "Violet was a special snowgirl. She always will be."

Jerzie bent down and picked up the soggy purple scarf.

Why did Mom say Violet will always be special? Jerzie wondered.

Violet is melted now. She is gone.

Jerzie and Josiah moped as they ate dinner.
Mom didn't tell Josiah to stop crying,
or tell Jerzie to cheer up.
Their sadness just seemed right.

Later, they snuggled up with Mom on her big, cozy bed.
Jerzie wore the purple scarf, now dry. She ran her fingers through the fringe.

Jerzie remembered the magical day when Violet came to be.
A smile slowly lit Jerzie's face. She looked to her brother.
"Remember pretending that Violet was Granddad, and he told
us that he was in love with Grandma?"

Josiah shrugged. But he lifted his eyes to meet Jerzie's.

"And," Jerzie continued, "Grandma kissed him on the cheek?"

"And," said Josiah, "Grandma said, 'Ooh, my lips are so cold!'"

That's when Jerzie realized it.
Her time with Violet had changed her.
Even though Violet was gone, she would
always be part of Jerzie.

Like Granddad.

And her birthday.

And the day she, Josiah, and Grandma built Violet.
Nothing could ever take away those memories.

Jerzie liked how those memories felt—like hidden treasure.
She took a deep breath, held on to Violet's scarf, and checked her feelings.
She felt grateful. She was glad she and Josiah and Grandma had
made Violet that special day.

Jerzie decided to draw a picture of Violet.
Of course, Josiah wanted to make one too.
When she finished her drawing, Jerzie
lifted her head and looked out the window.
She saw that the rain had turned to snow.

Jerzie smiled.

Tending to the Emotions of Children Experiencing Loss: A Guide for Caring Adults

Loss is part of life for all of us. Children can experience many types of loss, from moving homes or schools to the death of loved ones or pets to divorce. These losses may be difficult to handle. With help and safe places to discuss their emotions, children can learn skills to cope with their losses and manage their complex feelings.

Here are some important issues related to loss and grief raised in *Violet the Snowgirl*:

※ **Even during hard times, good things can happen.** If we know to look for them, we can enjoy them. When Jerzie woke up the day after her birthday, she expected it to be a bad day. It turned out to be a great day. Jerzie was excited to see the snow, and then to see her Grandma. It can be confusing to experience pleasant feelings, such as being happy, in the midst of grief. It may even cause guilt. Teaching children that it is okay to feel these pleasant feelings when they come along is an important source of support.

※ **We all need permission to be sad sometimes.** Both Josiah and Jerzie were sad when Violet melted. It was the end of something important to them. It's hard for adults to see children sad—but when adults acknowledge children's sadness, anger, or other uncomfortable emotions, this acknowledgment can allow them to feel that emotion and move on. Being with children through their uncomfortable feelings of loss, rather than encouraging them to feel something more pleasant, is validating for them. We can help children understand that their sadness will not last forever. But for as long as these uncomfortable feelings last, children have permission to feel them.

❋ **Children can learn to recognize their feelings.** The ability to identify emotions is a valuable skill for children to learn. Teaching them to reflect on how they feel, and giving them the language to express these feelings, helps them cope. Children are then able to figure out which coping skills to use and what help they can ask for. In *Violet the Snowgirl*, Jerzie takes deep breaths and checks her feelings.

❋ **Grieving is hard work.** It is a big, important task that takes a lot of energy for children and adults alike. Some things that helped Jerzie and Josiah deal with their sadness were being with their loved ones, talking about and drawing memories, and having a chance to experience their feelings and talk about them. Keep in mind that children may sometimes need extra support, such as from a counselor, social worker, or therapist. Remember—and help children understand—that people grieve loss in many different ways, and that's okay.

The feelings and experiences of Jerzie and Josiah can apply to many other types of losses. After reading *Violet the Snowgirl*, you can help children process important losses by asking them all or some of the following questions. Please feel free to use the story and modify the questions to best fit the needs of the children with whom you are working. Here's one question that can be helpful for processing all kinds of loss:

❋ At the end of the story, Jerzie checked her feelings and discovered that she felt grateful. Can you think of any reasons to be grateful even in this hard time?

MOVING

❋ What were some good things that happened to Jerzie on the day after her birthday?

❋ At the end of the story, Jerzie felt both sad that Violet melted and happy that she had time with the snowgirl. Have you ever had more than one feeling about the same thing? What are some examples of that? What are some feelings you have about moving? (This is a good time to use the Loss Wheel.)

❋ What good things do you think you might find in your new home or school?

❋ What are some things you will miss about your old home or school?

❋ Who are some people that you can talk to about this big change? (This is a good time to use the Circles of Support.)

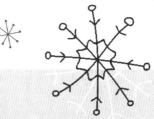

LOSS WHEEL

Draw your own loss wheel, photocopy the one on this page, or print a copy at freespirit.com/wheel. Tell the child, "For each feeling shown in this wheel, think about how much of your emotions that feeling is taking up. Starting in the center and working outward, color in the wedge to show the size of that feeling." Talk about the size of each feeling. Do this regularly. Notice how the child's feelings change over time. Many children like to fill out the Loss Wheel weekly and look at the changes. For some kids, it is a more intense process done less frequently, such as once a month.

Do I feel . . .

. . . shock? Am I still surprised?

. . . guilt? Do I feel like this is my fault?

. . . sorrow? Am I sad?

. . . anger? Am I mad?

. . . acceptance? Do I feel like I'm going to be okay?

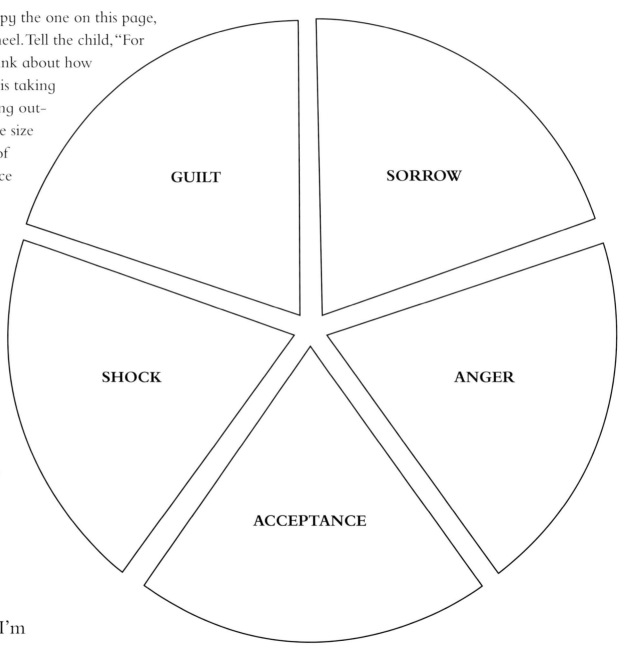

CIRCLES OF SUPPORT

Prompt the child, "Ask yourself, 'Who cares about me?' Think about family members, teachers and school staff, friends, pets, neighbors, and other friendly and caring grownups."

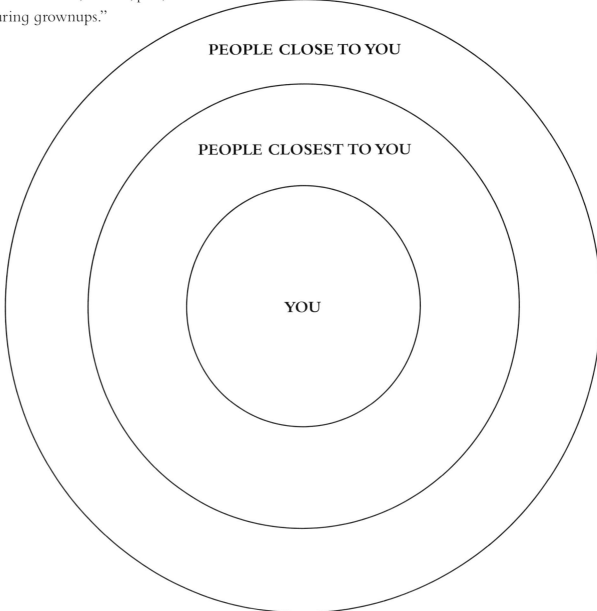

DEATH OF A PET

❈ It is hard to say good-bye to something you care a lot about. What was it like for Josiah and Jerzie to lose Violet? What would they miss about Violet?

❈ What will you miss about your pet?

❈ What are some of your best memories of your pet?

❈ How did Jerzie figure out how she was feeling?

❈ What feelings are you having? (This is a good time to use the Loss Wheel.)

❈ Who can you talk to about your feelings? (This is a good time to use the Circles of Support.)

❈ Jerzie and Josiah found it helpful to share memories of their snowgirl, even though they wouldn't see Violet again. Do you have any memories of your pet you would like to share? Would you like to draw a special picture of your pet?

DIVORCE

❈ Neither Jerzie nor Josiah wanted Violet to melt, but she melted anyway. What do you think that was like for them?

❈ Josiah had strong feelings of anger, and Jerzie of sadness, when Violet melted. When might you have these feelings? Are there other feelings that you might be having? (This is a good time to use the Loss Wheel.)

❈ What are some changes your family is going through that seem scary to you?

❈ Can you think of any changes that might be okay? If so, what are those?

❈ Jerzie and Josiah talked to their mom when they were sad about Violet. Who can you talk to about your feelings? (This is a good time to use the Circles of Support.)

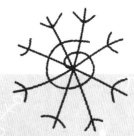

DEATH OF A LOVED ONE

❋ When Violet melted, Jerzie and Josiah had strong feelings. How do you think Josiah felt? Jerzie?

❋ After Violet melted, Josiah said, "I hate that snowgirl." Do you think he really hated her? Why do you think he might have said that?

❋ Sometimes when we are angry, we say things we don't really mean. Have you ever done that?

❋ What did Mom do after Josiah said he hated Violet? Why do you think she didn't tell him to stop crying?

❋ What did Jerzie do at the very end to make herself feel better? (She spent time with her family, talked about Violet, and drew a picture of Violet.) How do you think that helped? (This is a good time to use the Circles of Support.)

❋ When someone you love dies, you can feel some strong feelings. Sometimes you might feel mad. Sometimes sad. Can you tell me about the feelings you are having? (This is a good time to use the Loss Wheel.)

❋ You might have a lot of questions. What questions do you have?

❋ Jerzie and Josiah found it helpful to share memories of Violet, even though they wouldn't see her again. Do you have any memories you would like to share? Would you like to draw a special picture of your loved one?

❋ Several times, the story mentioned Granddad, who had died. What are some ways that Grandma, Jerzie, and Josiah kept Granddad's memory alive?

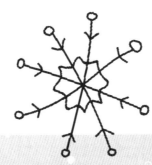

About the Author and Illustrator

LISA L. WALSH is a school social worker with more than twenty years of experience in counseling students from preschool to high school. She is the author of a young adult novel about a family affected by addiction. Her students inspired *Violet the Snowgirl*—it was a real-life discussion of loss in a classroom of eight-year-olds who were empathizing with a classmate whose father had been diagnosed with terminal cancer. Walsh has two adult daughters and lives in Gifford, Illinois.

WENDY LEACH was born in the heartland of the United States and has very stubbornly stayed put. Her love for picture book illustration grew while she was earning her BFA and working in the children's department of her local Barnes & Noble. Her favorite subjects to draw include cute kids and their pets, city landscapes, and lush garden spaces. She is a proud member of the Society of Children's Book Writers and Illustrators and was honored to be a featured illustrator on their website. She lives in Kansas City.

Other Great Books from Free Spirit

Sometimes When I'm Sad
by Deborah Serani, Psy.D.,
illustrated by Kyra Teis

For ages 4–8. 40 pp.; HC; full-color; 8¼" x 9".

I'm Happy-Sad Today
Making Sense of
Mixed-Together Feelings
by Lory Britain, Ph.D.,
illustrated by Matthew Rivera

For ages 3–8. 40 pp.; HC;
full-color; 11¼" x 9¼".

Feeling Sad!
by Kay Barnham,
illustrated by Mike Gordon

For ages 5–9. 32 pp.; HC; full-color; 7½" x 8¼".

Free Leader's Guide
freespirit.com/leader

1-2-3 My Feelings and Me
by Goldie Millar and Lisa A. Berger,
illustrated by Priscilla Burris

For ages 3–8. 40 pp.; HC;
full-color; 11¼" x 9¼".

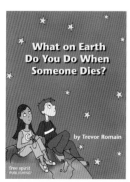

What on Earth Do You Do When Someone Dies?
by Trevor Romain

For ages 5–10. 72 pp.; PB; illust.; 5" x 7".

Interested in purchasing multiple quantities and receiving volume discounts?
Contact edsales@freespirit.com or call 1.800.735.7323 and ask for Education Sales.

Many Free Spirit authors are available for speaking engagements, workshops, and keynotes.
Contact speakers@freespirit.com or call 1.800.735.7323.

For pricing information, to place an order, or to request a free catalog, contact:

Free Spirit Publishing Inc.
6325 Sandburg Road • Suite 100 • Minneapolis, MN 55427-3674
toll-free 800.735.7323 • local 612.338.2068 • fax 612.337.5050
help4kids@freespirit.com • freespirit.com